The Phantom Tollbooth

A CHILDREN'S PLAY IN TWO ACTS

by Susan Nanus

Based on the Book
by Norton Juster

A SAMUEL FRENCH ACTING EDITION

New York Hollywood London Toronto
SAMUELFRENCH.COM

ISBN **978-0-573-65096-3** Printed in U.S.A. **#18004**

CAST

(in order of appearance)

(Maximum of 37 roles for 19 performers.)

THE CLOCK
MILO, a boy
THE WHETHER MAN
SIX LETHARGARIANS
TOCK, the WATCHDOG (same as THE CLOCK)
AZAZ THE UNABRIDGED, KING OF DICTIONOPOLIS
THE MATHEMAGICIAN, KING OF DIGITOPOLIS
PRINCESS SWEET RHYME
PRINCESS PURE REASON
GATEKEEPER OF DICTIONOPOLIS
THREE WORD MERCHANTS
THE LETTERMAN (FOURTH WORD MERCHANT)
SPELLING BEE
THE HUMBUG
THE DUKE OF DEFINITION
THE MINISTER OF MEANING
THE EARL OF ESSENCE
THE COUNT OF CONNOTATION
THE UNDERSECRETARY OF UNDERSTANDING
A PAGE
KAKAFONOUS A. DISCHORD, DOCTOR OF DISSONANCE
THE AWFUL DYNNE
THE DODECAHEDRON
MINERS OF THE NUMBERS MINE
THE EVERPRESENT WORDSNATCHER
THE TERRIBLE TRIVIUM
THE DEMON OF INSINCERITY
SENSES TAKER

SUGGESTED DOUBLING-UP OF ROLES

The six Lethargarians may serve as a chorus that plays all the smaller roles throughout the play. I would suggest that the Ministers of King Azaz's Cabinet be played by separate actors, but they also, may be played by the Lethargarian chorus.

Several other small parts may be played by the same actor, as well. The following is a suggested division of roles.

THE CLOCK, TOCK .... 1 actor

MILO .... 1 actor

THE WHETHER MAN, GATEKEEPER OF DICTIONOPOLIS, THE DODECAHEDRON .... 1 actor

LETHARGARIAN #1, WORD MERCHANT #1, THE EVERPRESENT WORDSNATCHER ...... 1 actor

LETHARGARIAN #2, WORD MERCHANT #2, THE TERRIBLE TRIVIUM .... 1 actor

LETHARGARIAN #3, WORD MERCHANT #3, THE DEMON OF INSINCERITY .... 1 actor

LETHARGARIAN #4, THE LETTERMAN, THE SENSES TAKER .... 1 actor

LETHARGARIAN #5, SPELLING BEE, a DEMON .. 1 actor

LETHARGARIAN #6, A PAGE, THE AWFUL DYNNE .... 1 actor

AZAZ THE UNABRIDGED .... 1 actor

THE MATHEMAGICIAN .... 1 actor

PRINCESS SWEET RHYME .... 1 actor

PRINCESS PURE REASON .... 1 actor

THE HUMBUG .... 1 actor

THE DUKE OF DEFINITION, KAKAFONOUS
A. DISCHORD .... 1 actor

THE MINISTER OF MEANING,
a NUMBERS MINER .... 1 actor

THE EARL OF ESSENCE, a NUMBERS MINER ... 1 actor

THE COUNT OF CONNOTATION,
a NUMBERS MINER .... 1 actor

THE UNDERSECRETARY OF UNDERSTANDING,
a NUMBERS MINER .... 1 actor

THE SET

It is recommended that the setting be either a platform set, employing vertical pipes from which banners, etc., are hung for various scenes, or a book set, with the spine UC, the leaves of the book being painted drops which are turned like book leaves whenever the scene changes.

The settings should be impressionistic rather than realistic:

1. Milo's bedroom—with shelves, pennants, pictures on the wall, as well as suggestions of the characters of the Land of Wisdom.

2. The road to the Land of Wisdom—a forest, from which the Whether Man and the Lethargarians emerge.

3. Dictionopolis—A marketplace full of open air stalls as well as little shops. Letters and signs should abound. There may be street signs and lampposts in the shapes of large letters (large O's and Q's) and all windows and doors can be in the shape of H's and A's.

4. Digitopolis—a dark, glittering place without trees or greenery, but full of shining rocks and cliffs, with hundreds of numbers shining everywhere. When the scene change is made to the Mathemagician's room, set pieces are simply carried in from the wings.

5. The Land of Ignorance—a grey, gloomy place full of cliffs and caves, with frightening faces. Different levels and heights should be suggested through one or two platforms or risers, with a set of stairs that lead to the castle in the air.

Pantomime and simple placards can be effective in the setting of a scene. Lighting is also important in helping differentiate one place from another.

Props and scenery should be two-dimensional and very colorful in order to give the effect of an imaginary place.

STAGE EFFECTS

The following are some suggestions as to how to create certain stage effects:

1. The movement of MILO's CAR can be simulated by setting the car in a permanent or fixed position and having the characters pantomime the movement of travel. They can sway, swing back and forth, and bump up and down to create the idea of riding in a car.

2. The appearance of the AWFUL DYNNE can occur in the wagon, so that Dynne merely pops out after the explosion. Or smoke can actually be used so that Dynne steps forward from the smoke.

3. All the SOUNDS or DR. DISCHORD can be recorded on tape.

4. The Attack of the Demons can be staged by using real actors who chase the heroes through the audience; or by projecting slides all over the walls of the theatre, accompanied by recorded sound effects; or through a pantomimed reaction by the heroes to what they see; or any other way the director can invent. The more invention in this play, the more fun.

The Phantom Tollbooth

ACT ONE

Scene 1

The stage is completely dark and silent. Suddenly the sound of someone winding an alarm clock is heard, and after that, the sound of loud ticking is heard.

LIGHTS UP on the Clock, *a huge alarm clock. The* Clock *reads 4:00. The lighting should make it appear that the* Clock *is suspended in mid-air (if possible). The* Clock *ticks for 30 seconds.*

Clock. See that! Half a minute gone by. Seems like a long time when you're waiting for something to happen, doesn't it? Funny thing is, time can pass very slowly or very fast, and sometimes even both at once. The time now? Oh, a little after four, but what that means should depend on you. Too often, we do something simply because time tells us to. Time for school, time for bed, whoops, 12:00, time to be hungry. It can get a little silly, don't you think? Time is important, but it's what you do with it that makes it so. So my advice to you is to use it. Keep your eyes open and your ears perked. Otherwise it will pass before you know it, and you'll certainly have missed something!

Things have a habit of doing that, you know.
Being here one minute and gone the next.

In the twinkling of an eye.
In a jiffy.
In a flash!

I know a girl who yawned and missed a whole summer vacation. And what about that caveman who took a nap one afternoon, and woke up to find himself completely alone. You see, while *he* was sleeping, someone had invented the wheel and everyone had moved to the suburbs. And then of course, there is Milo. (*LIGHTS UP to reveal* MILO's *Bedroom. The* CLOCK *appears to be on a shelf in the room of a young boy—a room filled with books, toys, games, maps, papers, pencils, a bed, a desk. There is a dartboard with numbers and the face of the* MATHEMAGICIAN, *a bedspread made from* KING AZAZ's *cloak, a kite looking like the* SPELLING BEE, *a punching bag with the* HUMBUG's *face, as well as records, a television, a toy car, and a large box that is wrapped and has an envelope taped to the top. The sound of FOOTSTEPS is heard, and then enter* MILO *dejectedly. He throws down his books and coat, flops into a chair, and sighs loudly.*) Who never knows what to do with himself—not just sometimes, but always. When he's in school, he wants to be out, and when he's out, he wants to be in. (*During the following speech,* MILO *examines the various toys, tools, and other possessions in the room, trying them out and rejecting them.*) Wherever he is, he wants to be somewhere else—and when he gets there, so what. Everything is too much trouble or a waste of time. Books—he's already read them. Games—boring. T.V.—dumb. So what's left? Another long, boring afternoon. Unless he bothers to notice a very large package that happened to arrive today.

MILO. (*Suddenly notices the package. He drags him-*

self over to it, and disinterestedly reads the label.) "For Milo, who has plenty of time." Well, that's true. (*Sighs and looks at it.*) No. (*Walks away.*) Well . . . (*Comes back. Rips open envelope and reads.*)

A VOICE. "One genuine turnpike tollbooth, easily assembled at home for use by those who have never traveled in lands beyond."

MILO. Beyond what? (*Continues reading.*)

A VOICE. "This package contains the following items:" (MILO *pulls the items out of the box and sets them up as they are mentioned.*) "One (1) genuine turnpike tollbooth to be erected according to directions. Three (3) precautionary signs to be used in a precautionary fashion. Assorted coins for paying tolls. One (1) map, strictly up to date, showing how to get from here to there. One (1) book of rules and traffic regulations which may not be bent or broken. Warning! Results are not guaranteed. If not perfectly satisfied, your wasted time will be refunded."

MILO. (*Skeptically.*) Come off it, who do you think you're kidding? (*Walks around and examines tollbooth.*) What am I supposed to do with this? (*The ticking of the* CLOCK *grows loud and impatient.*) Well . . . what else do I have to do. (MILO *gets into his toy car and drives up to the first sign. NOTE: The car may be an actual toy car propelled by pedals or a small motor, or simply a cardboard imitation that* MILO *can fit into, and move by walking.*)

VOICE. "HAVE YOUR DESTINATION IN MIND."

MILO. (*Pulls out the map.*) Now, let's see. That's funny. I never heard of any of these places. Well, it doesn't matter anyway. Dictionopolis. That's a weird name. I might as well go there. (*Begins to move, following map. Drives off.*)

CLOCK. See what I mean? You never know how

things are going to get started. But when you're bored, what you need more than anything is a rude awakening.

(*The ALARM goes off very loudly as the stage darkens. The sound of the alarm is transformed into the honking of a car horn, and is then joined by the blasts, bleeps, roars and growls of heavy highway traffic. When the lights come up,* MILO's *bedroom is gone and we see a lonely road in the middle of nowhere.*)

ACT ONE

SCENE 2

THE ROAD TO DICTIONOPOLIS.

ENTER MILO *in his car.*

MILO. This is weird! I don't recognize any of this scenery at all. (*A SIGN is held up before* MILO, *startling him.*) Huh? (*Reads.*) WELCOME TO EXPECTATIONS. INFORMATION, PREDICTIONS AND ADVICE CHEERFULLY OFFERED. PARK HERE AND BLOW HORN. (MILO *blows horn.*)

WHETHER MAN. (*A little man wearing a long coat and carrying an umbrella pops up from behind the sign that he was holding. He speaks very fast and excitedly.*) My, my, my, my, my, welcome, welcome, welcome, welcome to the Land of Expectations, Expectations, Expectations! We don't get many travelers these days; we certainly don't get many travelers. Now what can I do for you? I'm the Whether Man.

MILO. (*Referring to map.*) Uh . . . is this the right road to Dictionopolis?

WHETHER MAN. Well now, well now, well now, I don't know of any *wrong* road to Dictionopolis, so if this road goes to Dictionopolis at all, it must be the right road, and if it doesn't, it must be the right road to somewhere else, because there are no wrong roads to anywhere. Do you think it will rain?

MILO. I thought you were the Weather Man.

WHETHER MAN. Oh, no, I'm the Whether Man, not the weather man. (*Pulls out a SIGN or opens a FLAP of his coat, which reads: "WHETHER".*) After all, it's more important to know whether there will be weather than what the weather will be.

MILO. What kind of place is Expectations?

WHETHER MAN. Good question, good question! Expectations is the place you must always go to before you get to where you are going. Of course, some people never go beyond Expectations, but my job is to hurry them along whether they like it or not. Now what else can I do for you? (*Opens his umbrella.*)

MILO. I think I can find my own way.

WHETHER MAN. Splendid, splendid, splendid! Whether or not you find your own way, you're bound to find some way. If you happen to find my way, please return it. I lost it years ago. I imagine by now it must be quite rusty. You did say it was going to rain, didn't you? (*Escorts* MILO *to the car under the open umbrella.*) I'm glad you made your own decision. I do so hate to make up my mind about anything, whether it's good or bad, up or down, rain or shine. Expect everything. I always say, and the unexpected never happens. Goodbye, goodbye, goodbye, good . . . (*A loud CLAP of THUNDER is heard.*) Oh dear! (*He looks up at the sky, puts out his hand to feel fo·

rain, and RUNS AWAY. MILO *watches puzzledly and drives on.*)

MILO. I'd better get out of Expectations, but fast. Talking to a guy like that all day would get me nowhere for sure. (*He tries to speed up, but finds instead that he is moving slower and slower.*) Oh, oh, now what? (*He can barely move. Behind* MILO, *the* LETHARGARIANS *begin to enter from all parts of the stage. They are dressed to blend in with the scenery and carry small pillows that look like rocks. Whenever they fall asleep, they rest on the pillows.*) Now I really am getting nowhere. I hope I didn't take a wrong turn. (*The car stops. He tries to start it. It won't move. He gets out and begins to tinker with it.*) I wonder where I am.

LETHARGARIAN 1. You're . . . in . . . the . . . Dol . . . drums . . . (MILO *looks around.*)

LETHARGARIAN 2. Yes . . . the . . . Dol . . . drums . . . (*A YAWN is heard.*)

MILO. (*Yelling.*) WHAT ARE THE DOLDRUMS?

LETHARGARIAN 3. The Doldrums, my friend, are where nothing ever happens and nothing ever changes. (*Parts of the Scenery Stand Up or Six People come out of the scenery colored in the same colors of the trees or the road. They move very slowly and as soon as they move, they stop to rest again.*) Allow me to introduce all of us. We are the Lethargarians at your service.

MILO. (*Uncertainly.*) Very pleased to meet you. I think I'm lost. Can you help me?

LETHARGARIAN 4. Don't say think. (*He yawns.*) It's against the law.

LETHARGARIAN 1. No one's allowed to think in the Doldrums. (*He falls asleep.*)

LETHARGARIAN 2. Don't you have a rule book? It's local ordinance 175389-J. (*He falls asleep.*)

MILO. (*Pulls out rule book and reads.*) Ordinance 175389-J: "It shall be unlawful, illegal and unethical to think, think of thinking, surmise, presume, reason, meditate or speculate while in the Doldrums. Anyone breaking this law shall be severely punished." That's a ridiculous law! Everybody thinks.

ALL THE LETHARGARIANS. We don't!

LETHARGARIAN 2. And the most of the time, you don't, that's why you're here. You weren't thinking and you weren't paying attention either. People who don't pay attention often get stuck in the Doldrums. Face it, most of the time, you're just like us. (*Falls, snoring, to the ground.* MILO *laughs.*)

LETHARGARIAN 5. Stop that at once. Laughing is against the law. Don't you have a rule book? It's local ordinance 574381-W.

MILO. (*Opens rule book and reads.*) "In the Doldrums, laughter is frowned upon and smiling is permitted only on alternate Thursdays." Well, if you can't laugh or think, what can you do?

LETHARGARIAN 6. Anything as long as it's nothing, and everything as long as it isn't anything. There's lots to do. We have a very busy schedule . . .

LETHARGARIAN 1. At 8:00 we get up and then we spend from 8 to 9 daydreaming.

LETHARGARIAN 2. From 9:00 to 9:30 we take our early midmorning nap . . .

LETHARGARIAN 3. From 9:30 to 10:30 we dawdle and delay . . .

LETHARGARIAN 4. From 10:30 to 11:30 we take our late early morning nap . . .

LETHARGARIAN 5. From 11:30 to 12:00 we bide our time and then we eat our lunch.

LETHARGARIAN 6. From 1:00 to 2:00 we linger and loiter . . .

LETHARGARIAN 1. From 2:00 to 2:30 we take our early afternoon nap . . .

LETHARGARIAN 2. From 2:30 to 3:30 we put off for tomorrow what we could have done today . . .

LETHARGARIAN 3. From 3:30 to 4:00 we take our early late afternoon nap . . .

LETHARGARIAN 4. From 4:00 to 5:00 we loaf and lounge until dinner . . .

LETHARGARIAN 5. From 6:00 to 7:00 we dilly-dally . . .

LETHARGARIAN 6. From 7:00 to 8:00 we take our early evening nap and then for an hour before we go to bed, we waste time.

LETHARGARIAN 1. (*Yawning.*) You see, it's really quite strenuous doing nothing all day long, and so once a week, we take a holiday and go nowhere.

LETHARGARIAN 5. Which is just where we were going when you came along. Would you care to join us?

MILO. (*Yawning.*) That's where I seem to be going, anyway. (*Stretching.*) Tell me, does everyone here do nothing?

LETHARGARIAN 3. Everyone but the terrible watch-dog. He's always sniffing around to see that nobody wastes time. A most unpleasant character.

MILO. The Watchdog?

LETHARGARIAN 6. THE WATCHDOG!

ALL THE LETHARGARIANS. (*Yelling at once.*) RUN! WAKE UP! RUN! HERE HE COMES! THE WATCHDOG! (*They all run off and ENTER a large dog with the head, feet, and tail of a dog, and the body of a clock, having the same face as the character* THE CLOCK.)

WATCHDOG. What are you doing here?

MILO. Nothing much. Just killing time. You see . . .

WATCHDOG. KILLING TIME! (*His ALARM RINGS in fury.*) It's bad enough wasting time without killing it. What are you doing in the Doldrums, anyway? Don't you have anywhere to go?

MILO. I think I was on my way to Dictionopolis when I got stuck here. Can you help me?

WATCHDOG. Help you! You've got to help yourself. I suppose you know why you got stuck.

MILO. I guess I just wasn't thinking.

WATCHDOG. Precisely. Now you're on your way.

MILO. I am?

WATCHDOG. Of course. Since you got here by not thinking, it seems reasonable that in order to get out, you must *start* thinking. Do you mind if I get in? I love automobile rides. (*He gets in. They wait.*) Well?

MILO. All right. I'll try. (*Screws up his face and thinks.*) Are we moving?

WATCHDOG. Not yet. Think harder.

MILO. I'm thinking as hard as I can.

WATCHDOG. Well, think just a little harder than that. Come on, you can do it.

MILO. All right, all right. . . . I'm thinking of all the planets in the solar system, and why water expands when it turns to ice, and all the words that begin with "q," and . . . (*The wheels begin to move.*) We're moving! We're moving!

WATCHDOG. Keep thinking.

MILO. (*Thinking.*) How a steam engine works and how to bake a pie and the difference between Farenheit and Centigrade . . .

WATCHDOG. Dictionopolis, here we come.

MILO. Hey, Watchdog, are you coming along?

TOCK. You can call me Tock, and keep your eyes on the road.

MILO. What kind of place is Dictionopolis, anyway?

TOCK. It's where all the words in the world come from. It used to be a marvelous place, but ever since Rhyme and Reason left, it hasn't been the same.

MILO. Rhyme and Reason?

TOCK. The two princesses. They used to settle all the arguments between their two brothers who rule over the Land of Wisdom. You see, Azaz is the king of Dictionopolis and the Mathemagician is the king of Digitopolis and they almost never see eye to eye on anything. It was the job of the Princesses Sweet Rhyme and Pure Reason to solve the differences between the two kings, and they always did so well that both sides usually went home feeling very satisfied. But then, one day, the kings had an argument to end all arguments. . . .

(*The LIGHTS DIM on* TOCK *and* MILO, *and come up on* KING AZAZ *of Dictionopolis on another part of the stage.* AZAZ *has a great stomach, a grey beard reaching to his waist, a small crown and a long robe with the letters of the alphabet written all over it.*)

AZAZ. Of course, I'll abide by the decision of Rhyme and Reason, though I have no doubt as to what it will be. They will chose *words,* of course. Everyone knows that words are more important than numbers any day of the week.

(*The* MATHEMAGICIAN *appears opposite* AZAZ. *The* MATHEMAGICIAN *wears a long flowing robe covered entirely with complex mathematical equations, and a tall pointed hat. He carries a long staff with a pencil point at one end and a large rubber eraser at the other.*)

MATHEMAGICIAN. That's what you think, Azaz. People wouldn't even know what day of the week it is without *numbers*. Haven't you ever looked at a calendar? Face it, Azaz. It's numbers that count.

AZAZ. Don't be ridiculous. (*To audience, as if leading a cheer.*) Let's hear it for WORDS!

MATHEMAGICIAN. (*To audience, in the same manner.*) Cast your vote for NUMBERS!

AZAZ. A, B, C's!

MATHEMAGICIAN. 1, 2, 3's! (*A FANFARE is heard.*)

AZAZ AND MATHEMAGICIAN. (*To each other.*) Quiet! Rhyme and Reason are about to announce their decision.

(RHYME *and* REASON *appear.*)

RHYME. Ladies and gentlemen, letters and numeral, fractions and punctuation marks--may we have your attention, please. After careful consideration of the problem set before us by King Azaz of Dictionopolis (AZAZ *bows.*) and the Mathemagician of Digitopolis (MATHEMAGICIAN *raises his hands in a victory salute.*) we have come to the following conclusion:

REASON. Words and numbers are of equal value, for in the cloak of knowledge, one is the warp and the other is the woof.

RHYME. It is no more important to count the sands than it is to name the stars.

RHYME AND REASON. Therefore, let both kingdoms, Dictionopolis and Digitopolis live in peace.

(*The sound of CHEERING is heard.*)

AZAZ. Boo! is what I say. Boo and Bah and Hiss!

MATHEMAGICIAN. What good are these girls if they can't even settle an argument in anyone's favor? I think I have come to a decision of my own.

AZAZ. So have I.

AZAZ AND MATHEMAGICIAN. (*To the* PRINCESSES.) You are hereby banished from this land to the Castle-in-the-Air. (*To each other.*) And as for you, KEEP OUT OF MY WAY! (*They stalk off in opposite directions.*)

(*During this time, the set has been changed to the Market Square of Dictionopolis. LIGHTS come UP on the deserted square.*)

TOCK. And ever since then, there has been neither Rhyme nor Reason in this kingdom. Words are misused and numbers are mismanaged. The argument between the two kings has divided everyone and the real value of both words and numbers has been forgotten. What a waste!

MILO. Why doesn't somebody rescue the Princesses and set everything straight again?

TOCK. That is easier said than done. The Castle-in-the-Air is very far from here, and the one path which leads to it is guarded by ferocious demons. But hold on, here we are. (*A Man appears, carrying a Gate and a small Tollbooth.*)

GATEKEEPER. AHHHHREMMMM! This is Dictionopolis, a happy kingdom, advantageously located in the foothills of Confusion and caressed by gentle breezes from the Sea of Knowledge. Today, by royal proclamation, is Market Day. Have you come to buy or sell?

MILO. I beg your pardon?

GATEKEEPER. Buy or sell, buy or sell. Which is it? You must have come here for a reason.

MILO. Well, I . . .

GATEKEEPER. Come now, if you don't have a reason, you must at least have an explanation or certainly an excuse.

MILO. (*Meekly.*) Uh . . . no.

GATEKEEPER. (*Shaking his head.*) Very serious. You can't get in without a reason. (*Thoughtfully.*) Wait a minute. Maybe I have an old one you can use. (*Pulls out an old suitcase from the tollbooth and rummages through it.*) No . . . no . . . no . . . this won't do . . . hmmm . . .

MILO. (*To* TOCK.) What's he looking for? (TOCK *shrugs.*)

GATEKEEPER. Ah! This is fine. (*Pulls out a Medallion on a chain. Engraved in the Medallion is: "WHY NOT?"*) Why not. That's a good reason for almost anything . . . a bit used, perhaps, but still quite serviceable. There you are, sir. Now I can truly say: Welcome to Dictionopolis.

(*He opens the Gate and walks off. CITIZENS and MERCHANTS appear on all levels of the stage, and* MILO *and* TOCK *find themselves in the middle of a noisy marketplace. As some people buy and sell their wares, others hang a large banner which reads: WELCOME TO THE WORD MARKET.*)

MILO. Tock! Look!

MERCHANT 1. Hey-ya, hey-ya, hey-ya, step right up and take your pick. Juicy tempting words for sale. Get your fresh-picked "if's," "and's" and "but's!" Just take a look at these nice ripe "where's" and "when's."

MERCHANT 2. Step right up, step right up, fancy, best-quality words here for sale. Enrich your vocabulary and expand your speech with such elegant items as "quagmire," "flabbergast," or "upholstery."

MERCHANT 3. Words by the bag, buy them over here. Words by the bag for the more talkative customer. A pound of "happy's" at a very reasonable price . . . very useful for "Happy Birthday," "Happy New Year," "happy days," or "happy-go-lucky." Or how about a package of "good's," always handy for "good morning," "good afternoon," "good evening," and "goodbye."

MILO. I can't believe it. Did you ever see so many words?

TOCK. They're fine if you have something to say. (*They come to a Do-It-Yourself Bin.*)

MILO. (*To* MERCHANT 4 *at the Bin.*) Excuse me, but what are these?

MERCHANT 4. These are for people who like to make up their own words. You can pick any assortment you like or buy a special box complete with all the letters and a book of instructions. Here, taste an "A." They're very good. (*He pops one into* MILO's *mouth.*)

MILO. (*Tastes it hesitantly.*) It's sweet! (*He eats it.*)

MERCHANT 4. I knew you'd like it. "A" is one of our best-sellers. All of them aren't that good, you know. The "Z," for instance—very dry and sawdusty. And the "X?" Tastes like a trunkful of stale air. But most of the others aren't bad at all. Here, try the "I."

MILO. (*Tasting.*) Cool! It tastes icy.

MERCHANT 4. (*To* TOCK.) How about the "C" for you? It's as crunchy as a bone. Most people are just too lazy to make their own words, but take it from me, not only is it more fun, but it's also *de*-lightful, (*Holds *up a "D."*) *e*-lating, (*Holds up an "E."*) and extremely *u*seful! (*Holds up a "U."*)

MILO. But isn't it difficult? I'm not very good at making words.

(*The* SPELLING BEE, *a large colorful bee, comes up from behind.*)

SPELLING BEE. Perhaps I can be of some assistance . . . a-s-s-i-s-t-a-n-c-e. (*The Three turn around and see him.*) Don't be alarmed . . . a-l-a-r-m-e-d. I am the Spelling Bee. I can spell anything. Anything. A-n-y-t-h-i-n-g. Try me. Try me.

MILO. (*Backing off,* TOCK *on his guard.*) Can you spell goodbye?

SPELLING BEE. Perhaps you are under the misapprehension . . . m-i-s-a-p-p-r-e-h-e-n-s-i-o-n that I am dangerous. Let me assure you that I am quite peaceful. Now, think of the most difficult word you can, and I'll spell it.

MILO. Uh . . . o.k. (*At this point,* MILO *may turn to the audience and ask them to help him chose a word or he may think of one on his own.*) How about . . . "Curiosity?"

SPELLING BEE. (*Winking.*) Let's see now . . . uh . . . how much time do I have?

MILO. Just ten seconds. Count them off, Tock.

SPELLING BEE. (*As* TOCK *counts.*) Oh dear, oh dear. (*Just at the last moment, quickly.*) C-u-r-i-o-s-i-t-y.

MERCHANT 4. Correct! (ALL *Cheer.*)

MILO. Can you spell anything?

SPELLING BEE. (*Proudly.*) Just about. You see, years ago, I was an ordinary bee minding my own business, smelling flowers all day, occasionally picking up part-time work in people's bonnets. Then one day, I realized that I'd never amount to anything without an education, so I decided that . . .

HUMBUG. (*Coming up in a booming voice.*) BALDERDASH! (*He wears a lavish coat, striped pants, checked vest, spats and a derby hat.* Let me repeat . . . BALDERDASH! (*Swings his cane and clicks his heels in the air.*) Well, well, what have we here? Isn't someone going to introduce me to the little boy?

SPELLING BEE. (*Disdainfully.*) This is the Humbug. You can't trust a word he says.

HUMBUG. NONSENSE! Everyone can trust a Humbug. As I was saying to the king just the other day . . .

SPELLING BEE. You've never met the king. (*To* MILO.) Don't believe a thing he tells you.

HUMBUG. Bosh, my boy, pure bosh. The Humbugs are an old and noble family, honorable to the core. Why, we fought in the Crusades with Richard the Lionhearted, crossed the Atlantic with Columbus, blazed trails with the pioneers. History is full of Humbugs.

SPELLING BEE. A very pretty speech . . . s-p-e-e-c-h. Now, why don't you go away? I was just advising the lad of the importance of proper spelling.

HUMBUG. BAH! As soon as you learn to spell one word, they ask you to spell another. You can never catch up, so why bother? (*Puts his arm around* MILO.) Take my advice, boy, and forget about it. As my great-great-great-grandfather George Washington Humbug used to say . . .

SPELLING BEE. You, sir, are an imposter i-m-p-o-s-t-e-r who can't even spell his own name!

HUMBUG. What? You dare to doubt my word? The word of a Humbug? The word of a Humbug who has direct access to the ear of a King? And the king shall hear of this, I promise you . . .

VOICE 1. Did someone call for the king?

VOICE 2. Did you mention the monarch?

VOICE 3. Speak of the sovereign?

VOICE 4. Entreat the Emperor?

VOICE 5. Hail his highness?

(*Five tall, thin gentlemen regally dressed in silks and satins, plumed hats and buckeled shoes appear as they speak.*)

MILO. Who are they?

SPELLING BEE. The King's advisors. Or in more formal terms, his cabinet.

MINISTER 1. Greetings!

MINISTER 2. Salutations!

MINISTER 3. Welcome!

MINISTER 4. Good afternoon!

MINISTER 5. Hello!

MILO. Uh . . . Hi.

(*All the* MINISTERS, *from here on called by their numbers, unfold their scrolls and read in order.*)

MINISTER 1. By the order of Azaz the Unabridged . . .

MINISTER 2. King of Dictionopolis . . .

MINISTER 3. Monarch of letters . . .

MINISTER 4. Emperor of phrases, sentences, and miscellaneous figures of speech . . .

MINISTER 5. We offer you the hospitality of our kingdom . . .

MINISTER 1. Country

MINISTER 2. Nation

MINISTER 3. State

MINISTER 4. Commonwealth

MINISTER 5. Realm

MINISTER 1. Empire

MINISTER 2. Palatinate

MINISTER 3. Principality.

MILO. Do all those words mean the same thing?

MINISTER 1. Of course.

MINISTER 2. Certainly.

MINISTER 3. Precisely.

MINISTER 4. Exactly.

MINISTER 5. Yes.

MILO. Then why don't you use just one? Wouldn't that make a lot more sense?

MINISTER 1. Nonsense!

MINISTER 2. Ridiculous!

MINISTER 3. Fantastic!

MINISTER 4. Absurd!

MINISTER 5. Bosh!

MINISTER 1. We're not interested in making sense. It's not our job.

MINISTER 2. Besides, one word is as good as another, so why not use them all?

MINISTER 3. Then you don't have to choose which one is right.

MINISTER 4. Besides, if one is right, then ten are ten times as right.

MINISTER 5. Obviously, you don't know who we are. (*Each presents himself and* MILO *acknowledges the introduction.*)

MINISTER 1. The Duke of Definition.

MINISTER 2. The Minister of Meaning.

MINISTER 3. The Earl of Essence.

MINISTER 4. The Count of Connotation.

MINISTER 5. The Undersecretary of Understanding.

ALL FIVE. And we have come to invite you to the Royal Banquet.

SPELLING BEE. The banquet! That's quite an honor, my boy. A real h-o-n-o-r.

HUMBUG. DON'T BE RIDICULOUS! Everybody goes to the Royal Banquet these days.

SPELLING BEE. (*To the* HUMBUG.) True, everybody does go. But some people are invited and others simply push their way in where they aren't wanted.

HUMBUG. HOW DARE YOU? You buzzing little upstart, I'll show you who's not wanted . . . (*Raises his cane threateningly.*)

SPELLING BEE. You just watch it! I'm warning w-a-r-n-i-n-g you! (*At that moment, an ear-shattering blast of TRUMPETS, entirely off-key, is heard, and a* PAGE *appears.*)

PAGE. King Azaz the Unabridged is about to begin the Royal Banquet. All guests who do not appear promptly at the table will automatically lose their place. (*A huge Table is carried out with* KING AZAZ *sitting in a large chair, carried out at the head of the table.*)

AZAZ. Places. Everyone take your places. (*All the characters, including the* HUMBUG *and the* SPELLING BEE, *who forget their quarrel, rush to take their places at the table.* MILO *and* TOCK *sit near the* KING. AZAZ *looks at* MILO.) And just who is this?

MILO. Your Highness, my name is Milo and this is Tock. Thank you very much for inviting us to your banquet, and I think your palace is beautiful!

MINISTER 1. Exquisite.

MINISTER 2. Lovely.

MINISTER 3. Handsome.

MINISTER 4. Pretty.

MINISTER 5. Charming.

AZAZ. SILENCE! Now tell me, young man, what can you do to entertain us? Sing songs? Tell stories? Juggle plates? Do tumbling tricks? Which is it?

MILO. I can't do any of those things.

AZAZ. What an ordinary little boy. Can't you do anything at all?

MILO. Well . . . I can count to a thousand.

AZAZ. AARGH, numbers! Never mention numbers here. Only use them when we absolutely have to. Now, why don't we change the subject and have some dinner? Since you are the guest of honor, you may pick the menu.

MILO. Me? Well, uh . . . I'm not very hungry. Can we just have a light snack?

AZAZ. A light snack it shall be!

(AZAZ *claps his hands. Waiters rush in with covered trays. When they are uncovered, Shafts of Light pour out. The light may be created through the use of battery-operated flashlights which are secured in the trays and covered with a false bottom. The Guests help themselves.*)

HUMBUG. Not a very substantial meal. Maybe you can suggest something a little more filling.

MILO. Well, in that case, I think we ought to have a square meal . . .

AZAZ. (*Claps his hands.*) A square meal it is! (*Waiters serve trays of Colored Squares of all sizes. People serve themselves.*)

SPELLING BEE. These are awful. (HUMBUG *Coughs and all the Guests do not care for the food.*)

AZAZ. (*Claps his hands and the trays are removed.*) Time for speeches. (*To* MILO.) You first.

MILO. (*Hesitantly.*) Your Majesty, ladies and gentlemen, I would like to take this opportunity to say that . . .

AZAZ. That's quite enough. Musn't talk all day.

MILO. But I just started to . . .

AZAZ. NEXT!

HUMBUG. (*Quickly.*) Roast turkey, mashed potatoes, vanilla ice cream.

SPELLING BEE. Hamburgers, corn on the cob, chocolate pudding p-u-d-d-i-n-g. (*Each Guest names two dishes and a dessert.*)

AZAZ. (*The last.*) Pate de fois gras, soupe a l'oignon, salade endives, fromage et fruits et demi-tasse. (*He claps his hands. Waiters serve each Guest his Words.*) Dig on. (*To* MILO.) Though I can't say I think much of your choice.

MILO. I didn't know I was going to have to eat my words.

AZAZ. Of course, of course, everybody here does. Your speech should have been in better taste.

MINISTER 1. Here, try some somersault. It improves the flavor.

MINISTER 2. Have a rigamarole. (*Offers bread-basket.*)

MINISTER 3. Or a ragamuffin.

MINISTER 4. Perhaps you'd care for a synonym bun.

MINISTER 5. Why not wait for your just desserts?

AZAZ. Ah yes, the dessert. We're having a special treat today . . . freshly made at the half-bakery.

MILO. The half-bakery?

AZAZ. Of course, the half-bakery! Where do you think half-baked ideas come from? Now, please don't interrupt. By royal command, the pastry chefs have . . .

MILO. What's a half-baked idea?

(AZAZ *gives up the idea of speaking as a cart is wheeled in and the Guests help themselves.*)

HUMBUG. They're very tasty, but they don't always agree with you. Here's a good one. (HUMBUG *hands one to* MILO.)

MILO. (*Reads.*) "The earth is flat."

SPELLING BEE. People swallowed that one for years. (*Picks up one and reads.*) "The moon is made of green cheese." Now, there's a half-baked idea.

(*Everyone chooses one and eats. They include: "It Never Rains But Pours," "Night Air Is Bad Air," "Everything Happens For The Best," "Coffee Stunts Your Growth."*)

AZAZ. And now for a few closing words. Attention! Let me have your attention! (*Everyone leaps up and Exits, except for* MILO, TOCK *and the* HUMBUG.) Loyal subjects and friends, once again on this gala occasion, we have . . .

MILO. Excuse me, but everybody left.

AZAZ. (*Sadly.*) I was hoping no one would notice. It happens every time.

HUMBUG. They've gone to dinner, and as soon as I finish this last bite, I shall join them.

MILO. That's ridiculous. How can they eat dinner right after a banquet?

AZAZ. SCANDALOUS! We'll put a stop to it at once. From now on, by royal command, everyone must eat dinner before the banquet.

MILO. But that's just as bad.

HUMBUG. Or just as good. Things which are equally bad are also equally good. Try to look at the bright side of things.

MILO. I don't know which side of anything to look at. Everything is so confusing, and all your words only make things worse.

AZAZ. How true. There must be something we can do about it.

HUMBUG. Pass a law.

AZAZ. We have almost as many laws as words.

HUMBUG. Offer a reward. (AZAZ *shakes his head and looks madder at each suggestion.*) Send for help? Drive a bargain? Pull the switch? Lower the boom? Toe the line? (*As* AZAZ *continues to scowl, the* HUMBUG *loses confidence and finally gives up.*)

MILO. Maybe you should let Rhyme and Reason return.

AZAZ. How nice that would be. Even if they were a bother at times, things always went so well when they were here. But I'm afraid it can't be done.

HUMBUG. Certainly not. Can't be done.

MILO. Why not?

HUMBUG. (*Now siding with* MILO.) Why not, indeed?

AZAZ. Much too difficult.

HUMBUG. Of course, much too difficult.

MILO. You could, if you really wanted to.

HUMBUG. By all means, if you really wanted to, you could.

AZAZ. (*To* HUMBUG.) How?

MILO. (*Also to* HUMBUG.) Yeah, how?

HUMBUG. Why . . . uh, it's a simple task for a brave boy with a stout heart, a steadfast dog and a serviceable small automobile.

AZAZ. Go on.

HUMBUG. Well, all that he would have to do is cross the dangerous, unknown countryside between here and Digitopolis, where he would have to persuade the Mathemagician to release the Princesses, which we know to be impossible because the Mathemagician will never agree with Azaz about anything. Once achieving that, it's a simple matter of entering the Mountains of Ignorance from where no one has ever returned alive, an effortless climb up a two thousand foot stairway without railings in a high wind at night to the Castle-in-the-Air. After a pleasant chat with the Princesses, all that remains is a leisurely ride back through those chaotic crags where the frightening fiends have sworn to tear any intruder from limb to limb and devour him down to his belt buckle. And finally after doing all that, a triumphal parade! If, of course, there is anything left to parade . . . followed by hot chocolate and cookies for everyone.

AZAZ. I never realized it would be so simple.

MILO. It sounds dangerous to me.

TOCK. And just who is supposed to make that journey?

AZAZ. A very good question. But there is one far more serious problem.

MILO. What's that?

AZAZ. I'm afraid I can't tell you that until you return.

MILO. But wait a minute, I didn't . . .

AZAZ. Dictionopolis will always be grateful to you, my boy and your dog. (AZAZ *pats* TOCK *and* MILO.)

TOCK. Now, just one moment, sire . . .

AZAZ. You will face many dangers on your journey, but fear not, for I can give you something for your protection. (AZAZ *gives* MILO *a box.*) In this box are the letters of the alphabet. With them you can form all the words you will ever need to help you overcome the obstacles that may stand in your path. All you must do is use them well and in the right places.

MILO. (*Miserably.*) Thanks a lot.

AZAZ. You will need a guide, of course, and since he knows the obstacles so well, the Humbug has cheerfully volunteered to accompany you.

HUMBUG. Now, see here . . . !

AZAZ. You will find him dependable, brave, resourceful and loyal.

HUMBUG. (*Flattered.*) Oh, your Majesty.

MILO. I'm sure he'll be a great help. (*They approach the car.*)

TOCK. I hope so. It looks like we're going to need it.

(*The lights darken and the* KING *fades from view.*)

AZAZ. Good luck! Drive carefully! (*The three get into the car and begin to move. Suddenly a thunderously loud NOISE is heard. They slow down the car.*)

MILO. What was that?

TOCK. It came from up ahead.

HUMBUG. It's something terrible, I just know it. Oh, no. Something dreadful is going to happen to us. I can feel it in my bones. (*The NOISE is repeated. They all look at each other fearfully. As the lights fade.*)

END OF ACT ONE

ACT TWO

Scene 1

The set of Digitopolis glitters in the background, while Upstage Right near the road, a small colorful Wagon sits, looking quite deserted. On its side in large letters, a sign reads:
"KAKAFONOUS A. DISCHORD
Doctor of Dissonance"

ENTER Milo, Tock *and* Humbug, *fearfully. They look at the wagon.*

Tock. There's no doubt about it. That's where the noise was coming from.

Humbug. (*To* Milo.) Well, go on.

Milo. Go on what?

Humbug. Go on and see who's making all that noise in there. We can't just ignore a creature like that.

Milo. Creature? What kind of creature? Do you think he's dangerous?

Humbug. Go on, Milo. Knock on the door. We'll be right behind you.

Milo. O.K. Maybe he can tell us how much further it is to Digitopolis.

(Milo *tiptoes up to the wagon door and KNOCKS timidly. The moment he knocks, a terrible CRASH is heard inside the wagon, and* Milo *and the others jump back in fright. At the same time, the*

Door Flies Open, and from the dark interior, a Hoarse VOICE *inquires.*)

VOICE. Have you ever heard a whole set of dishes dropped from the ceiling onto a hard stone floor? (*The Others are speechless with fright.* MILO *shakes his head.* VOICE *happily.*) Have you ever heard an ant wearing fur slippers walk across a thick wool carpet? (MILO *shakes his head again.*) Have you ever heard a blindfolded octopus unwrap a celephane-covered bathtub? (MILO *shakes his head a third time.*) Ha! I knew it. (*He hops out, a little man, wearing a white coat, with a stethoscope around his neck, and a small mirror attached to his forehead, and with very huge ears, and a mortar and pestle in his hands. He stares at* MILO, TOCK *and* HUMBUG.) None of you looks well at all! Tsk, tsk, not at all. (*He opens the top or side of his Wagon, revealing a dusty interior resembling an old apothecary shop, with shelves lined with jars and boxes, a table, books, test tubes and bottles and measuring spoons.*)

MILO. (*Timidly.*) Are you a doctor?

DISCHORD. (VOICE.) I am KAKAFONOUS A. DISCHORD, DOCTOR OF DISSONANCE! (*Several small explosions and a grinding crash are heard.*)

HUMBUG. (*Stuttering with fear.*) What does the "A" stand for?

DISCHORD. *AS LOUD AS POSSIBLE!* (*Two screeches and a bump is heard.*) Now, step a little closer and stick out your tongues. (DISCHORD *examines them.*) Just as I expected. (*He opens a large dusty book and thumbs through the pages.*) You're all suffering from a severe lack of noise. (DISCHORD *begins running around, collecting bottles, reading the labels to himself as he goes along.*) "Loud Cries." "Soft Cries." "Bangs, Bongs, Swishes, Swooshes." "Snaps and Crackles." "Whistles and Gongs." "Squeeks, Squacks, and Miscellaneous Uproar." (*As he reads them off, he pours a little of each into a large glass beaker and stirs the mixture with a wooden spoon. The concoction smokes and bubbles.*) Be ready in just a moment.

MILO. (*Suspiciously.*) Just what kind of doctor are you?

DISCHORD. Well, you might say, I'm a specialist. I specialize in noises, from the loudest to the softest, and from the slightly annoying to the terribly unpleasant. For instance, have you ever heard a square-wheeled steamroller ride over a street full of hard-boiled eggs? (*Very loud CRUNCHING SOUNDS are heard.*)

MILO. (*Holding his ears.*) But who would want all those terrible noises?

DISCHORD. (*Surprised at the question.*) Everybody does. Why, I'm so busy I can hardly fill all the orders for noise pills, racket lotion, clamor salve and hubub tonic. That's all people seem to want these days. Years ago, everyone wanted pleasant sounds and business was terrible. But then the cities were built and there was a great need for honking horns, screeching trains, clanging bells and all the rest of those wonderfully unpleasant sounds we use so much today. I've been working overtime ever since and my medicine here is in great demand. All you have to do is take one spoonful every day, and you'll never have to hear another beautiful sound again. Here, try some.

HUMBUG. (*Backing away.*) If it's all the same to you, I'd rather not.

MILO. I don't want to be cured of beautiful sounds.

TOCK. Besides, there's no such sickness as a lack of noise.

DISCHORD. How true. That's what makes it so difficult to cure. (*Takes a large glass bottle from the shelf.*) Very well, if you want to go all through life suffering from a noise deficiency, I'll just give this to Dynne for his lunch. (*Uncorks the bottle and pours the liquid into it. There is a rumbling and then a loud explosion accompanied by smoke, out of which* DYNNE, *a smog-like creature with yellow eyes and a frowning mouth, appears.*)

DYNNE. (*Smacking his lips.*) Ahhh, that was good, Master. I thought you'd never let me out. It was really cramped in there.

DISCHORD. This is my assistant, the awful Dynne. You must forgive his appearance, for he really doesn't have any.

MILO. What is a Dynne?

DISCHORD. You mean you've never heard of the awful Dynne? When you're playing in your room and making a great amount of noise, what do they tell you to stop?

MILO. That awful din.

DISCHORD. When the neighbors are playing their radio too loud late at night, what do you wish they'd turn down?

TOCK. That awful din.

DISCHORD. And when the street on your block is being repaired and the drills are working all day, what does everyone complain of?

HUMBUG. (*Brightly.*) The dreadful row.

DYNNE. The Dreadful Rauw was my grandfather. He perished in the great silence epidemic of 1712. I certainly can't understand why you don't like noise.

Why, I heard an explosion last week that was so lovely, I groaned with appreciation for two days. (*He gives a loud groan at the memory.*)

DISCHORD. He's right, you know. Noise is the most valuable thing in the world.

MILO. King Azaz says words are.

DISCHORD. NONSENSE! Why, when a baby wants food, how does he ask?

DYNNE. (*Happily.*) He screams!

DISCHORD. And when a racing car wants gas?

DYNNE. (*Jumping for joy.*) It chokes!

DISCHORD. And what happens to the dawn when a new day begins?

DYNNE. (*Delighted.*) It breaks!

DISCHORD. You see how simple it is? (*To* DYNNE.) Isn't it time for us to go?

MILO. Where to? Maybe we're going the same way.

DYNNE. I doubt it. (*Picking up empty sacks from the table.*) We're going on our collection rounds. Once a day, I travel through out the kingdom and collect all the wonderfully horrible and beautifully unpleasant sounds I can find and bring them back to the doctor to use in his medicine.

DISCHORD. Where are you going?

MILO. To Digitopolis.

DISCHORD. Oh, there are a number of ways to get to Digitopolis, if you know how to follow directions. Just take a look at the sign at the fork in the road. Though why you'd ever want to go there, I'll never know.

MILO. We want to talk to the Mathemagician.

HUMBUG. About the release of the Princesses Rhyme and Reason.

DISCHORD. Rhyme and Reason? I remember them. Very nice girls, but a little too quiet for my taste. In fact, I've been meaning to send them something that Dynne brought home by mistake and which I have absolutely no use for. (*He rummages through the wagon.*) Ah, here it is . . . or maybe you'd like it for yourself. (*Hands* MILO *a package.*)

MILO. What is it?

DISCHORD. The sounds of laughter. They're so unpleasant to hear, it's almost unbearable. All those giggles and snickers and happy shouts of joy, I don't know what Dynne was thinking of when he collected them. Here, take them to the Princesses or keep them for yourselves, I don't care. Well, time to move on. Goodbye now and good luck! (*He has shut the wagon by now and gets in. LOUD NOISES begin to erupt as* DYNNE *pulls the wagon offstage.*)

MILO. (*Calling after them.*) But wait! The fork in the road . . . you didn't tell us where it is . . .

TOCK. It's too late. He can't hear a thing.

HUMBUG. I could use a fork of my own, at the moment. And a knife and a spoon to go with it. All of a sudden, I feel very hungry.

MILO. So do I, but it's no use thinking about it. There won't be anything to eat until we reach Digitopolis. (*They get into the car.*)

HUMBUG. (*Rubbing his stomach.*) Well, the sooner the better is what I say.

(*A SIGN suddenly appears.*)

VOICE. (*A strange voice from nowhere.*) But which way will get you there sooner? That is the question.

TOCK. Did you hear something?

MILO. Look! The fork in the road and a signpost to Digitopolis! (*They read the Sign.*)

DIGITOPOLIS

5	Miles
1,600	Rods
8,800	Yards
26,400	Feet
316,800	Inches
633,600	Half Inches

AND THEN SOME

HUMBUG. Let's travel by miles, it's shorter.

MILO. Let's travel by half inches. It's quicker.

TOCK. But which road should we take? It must make a difference.

MILO. Do you think so?

TOCK. Well, I'm not sure, but . . .

HUMBUG. He could be right. On the other hand, he could also be wrong. Does it make a difference or not?

VOICE. Yes, indeed, indeed it does, certainly, my yes, it does make a difference.

(*The* DODECAHEDRON *Appears, a 12-sides figure with a different face on each side, and with all the edges labeled with a small letter and all the angles labeled with a large letter. He wears a beret and peers at the others with a serious face. He doffs his cap and recites:*)

DODECAHEDRON.

My angles are many.
My sides are not few.
I'm the Dodecahedron.
Who are you?

MILO. What's a Dodecahedron?

DODECAHEDRON. (*Turning around slowly.*) See for yourself. A Dodecahedron is a mathematical shape with 12 faces. (*All his faces appear as he turns, each face with a different expression. He points to them.*) I usually use one at a time. It saves wear and tear. What are you called?

MILO. Milo.

DODECAHEDRON. That's an odd name. (*Changing his smiling face to a frowning one.*) And you have only one face.

MILO. (*Making sure it is still there.*) Is that bad?

DODECAHEDRON. You'll soon wear it out using it for everything. Is everyone with one face called Milo?

MILO. Oh, no. Some are called Billy or Jeffery or Sally or Lisa or lots of other things.

DODECAHEDRON. How confusing. Here everything is called exactly what it is. The triangles are called triangles, the circles are called circles, and even the same numbers have the same name. Can you imagine what would happen if we named all the twos Billy or Jeffery or Sally or Lisa or lots of other things? You'd have to say Robert plus John equals four, and if the fours were named Albert, things would be hopeless.

MILO. I never thought of it that way.

DODECAHEDRON. (*With an admonishing face.*) Then I suggest you begin at once, for in Digitopolis, everything is quite precise.

MILO. Then perhaps you can help us decide which road we should take.

DODECAHEDRON. (*Happily.*) By all means. There's nothing to it. (*As he talks, the three others try to solve the problem on a Large Blackboard that is wheeled onstage for the occasion.*) Now, if a small car carrying three people at 30 miles an hour for 10 minutes along a road 5 miles long at 11:35 in the morning starts at the same time as 3 people who have been traveling in a little automobile at 20 miles an hour for 15 minutes on another road exactly twice as long as half the disance of the other, while a dog, a bug, and a boy travel an equal distance in the same time or the same distance in an equal time along a third road in mid-October, then which one arrives first and which is the best way to go?

HUMBUG. Seventeen!

MILO. (*Still figuring frantically.*) I'm not sure, but . . .

DODECAHEDRON. You'll have to do better than that.

MILO. I'm not very good at problems.

DODECAHEDRON. What a shame. They're so very useful. Why, did you know that if a beaver 2 feet long with a tail a foot and a half long can build a dam 12 feet high and 6 feet wide in 2 days, all you would need to build Boulder Dam is a beaver 68 feet long with a 51 foot tail?

HUMBUG. (*Grumbling as his pencil snaps.*) Where would you find a beaver that big?

DODECAHEDRON. I don't know, but if you did, you'd certainly know what to do with him.

MILO. That's crazy.

DODECAHEDRON. That may be true, but it's completely accurate, and as long as the answer is right, who cares if the question is wrong?

TOCK. (*Who has been patiently doing the first problem.*) All three roads arrive at the same place at the same time.

DODECAHEDRON. Correct! And I'll take you there myself. (*The blackboard rolls off, and all four get into the car and drive off.*) Now you see how important problems are. If you hadn't done this one properly, you might have gone the wrong way.

MILO. But if all the roads arrive at the same place at the same time, then aren't they all the right road?

DODECAHEDRON. (*Glaring from his upset face.*) Certainly not! They're all the wrong way! Just because you have a choice, it doesn't mean that any of them *has* to be right. (*Pointing in another direction.*) That's the way to Digitopolis and we'll be there any moment. (*Suddenly the lighting grows dimmer.*) In fact, we're here. Welcome to the Land of Numbers.

HUMBUG. (*Looking around at the barren landscape.*) It doesn't look very inviting.

MILO. Is this the place where numbers are made?

DODECAHEDRON. They're not made. You have to dig for them. Don't you know anything at all about numbers?

MILO. Well, I never really thought they were very important.

DODECAHEDRON. NOT IMPORTANT! Could you have tea for two without the 2? Or three blind mice without the 3? And how would you sail the seven seas without the 7?

MILO. All I meant was . . .

DODECAHEDRON. (*Continues shouting angrily.*) If you had high hopes, how would you know how high they were? And did you know that narrow escapes come in different widths? Would you travel the whole world wide without ever knowing how wide it was? And how could you do anything at long last without knowing how long the last was? Why numbers are the most beautiful and valuable things in the world. Just follow me and I'll show you. (*He motions to them and pantomimes walking through rocky terrain with the others in tow. A Doorway similar to the Tollbooth ap-*

pears and the DODECAHEDRON *opens it and motions the others to follow him through.*) Come along, come along. I can't wait for you all day. (*They Enter the doorway and the lights are dimmed very low, as to simulate the interior of a cave. The SOUNDS of scrapings and tapping, scuffling and digging are heard all around them. He hands them Helmets with flashlights attached.*) Put these on.

MILO. (*Whispering.*) Where are we going?

DODECAHEDRON. We're here. This is the numbers mine. (*LIGHTS UP A LITTLE, revealing Little Men digging and chopping, shoveling and scraping.*) Right this way and watch your step. (*His voice echoes and reverberates. Irridescent and glittery numbers seem to sparkle from everywhere.*)

MILO. (*Awed.*) Whose mine is it?

VOICE OF MATHEMAGICIAN. By the four million eight hundred and twenty-seven thousand six hundred and fifty-nine hairs on my head, it's mine, of course! (*ENTER* THE MATHEMAGICIAN, *carrying his long staff which looks like a giant pencil.*)

HUMBUG. (*Already intimidated.*) It's a lovely mine, really it is.

MATHEMAGICIAN. (*Proudly.*) The biggest number mine in the kingdom.

MILO. (*Excitedly.*) Are there any precious stones in it?

MATHEMAGICIAN. *Precious stones!* (*Then softly.*) By the eight million two hundred and forty-seven thousand three hundred and twelve threads in my robe, I'll say there are. Look here. (*Reaches in a cart, pulls out a small object, polishes it vigorously and holds it to the light, where it sparkles.*)

MILO. But that's a five.

MATHEMAGICIAN. Exactly. As valuable a jewel as you'll find anywhere. Look at some of the others. (*Scoops up others and pours them into* MILO'S *arms. They include all numbers from 1 to 9 and an assortment of zeroes.*)

DODECAHEDRON. We dig them and polish them right here, and then send them all over the world. Marvelous, aren't they?

TOCK. They are beautiful. (*He holds them up to compare them to the numbers on his clock body.*)

MILO. So that's where they come from. (*Looks at them and carefully hands them back, but drops a few which smash and break in half.*) Oh, I'm sorry!

MATHEMAGICIAN. (*Scooping them up.*) Oh, don't worry about that. We use the broken ones for fractions. How about some lunch?

(*Takes out a little wihstle and blows it. Two miners rush in carrying an immense cauldron which is bubbling and steaming. The workers put down their tools and gather around to eat.*)

HUMBUG. That looks delicious! (TOCK *and* MILO *also look hungrily at the pot.*)

MATHEMAGICIAN. Perhaps you'd care for something to eat?

MILO. Oh, yes, sir!

TOCK. Thank you.

HUMBUG. (*Already eating.*) Ummm . . . delicious! (*All finish their bowls immediately.*)

MATHEMAGICIAN. Please have another portion. (*They eat and finish.* MATHEMAGICIAN *serves them again.*) Don't stop now. (*They finish.*) Come on, no need to be bashful. (*Serves them again.*)

MILO. (*To* TOCK *and* HUMBUG *as he finishes again.*) Do you want to hear something strange? Each one I eat makes me a little hungrier than before.

MATHEMAGICIAN. Do have some more. (*He serves them again. They eat frantically, until the* MATHEMAGICIAN *blows his whistle again and the pot is removed.*)

HUMBUG. (*Holding his stomach.*) Uggghhh! I think I'm starving.

MILO. Me, too, and I ate so much.

DODECAHEDRON. (*Wiping the gravy from several of his mouths.*) Yes, it was delicious, wasn't it? It's the specialty of the kingdom . . . subtraction stew.

TOCK. (*Weak from hunger.*) I have more of an appetite than when I began.

MATHEMAGICIAN. Certainly, what did you expect? The more you eat, the hungrier you get, everyone knows that.

MILO. They do? Then how do you get enough?

MATHEMAGICIAN. Enough? Here in Digitopolis, we have our meals when we're full and eat until we're hungry. That way, when you don't have anything at all, you have more than enough. It's a very economical system. You must have been stuffed to have eaten so much.

DODECAHEDRON. It's completely logical. The more you want, the less you get, and the less you get, the more you have. Simple arithmetic, that's all. (TOCK, MILO *and* HUMBUG *look at him blankly.*) Now, look, suppose you had something and added nothing to it. What would you have?

MILO. The same.

DODECAHEDRON. Splendid! And suppose you had something and added less than nothing to it? What would you have then?

HUMBUG. Starvation! Oh, I'm so hungry.

DODECAHEDRON. Now, now, it's not as bad as all that. In a few hours, you'll be nice and full again . . . just in time for dinner.

MILO. But I only eat when I'm hungry.

MATHEMAGICIAN. (*Waving the eraser of his staff.*) What a curious idea. The next thing you'll have us believe is that you only sleep when you're tired.

(*The mine has disappeared as well as the Miners. This may be done by dropping a curtain in front of the mine, through a blackout on the stage, while a single spotlight remains on the* MATHEMAGICIAN *and the others, or through the use of multi-level platforms. The Miners may fall behind the platforms, as two-dimensional props which depict the* MATHEMAGICIAN'S *Room are dropped down or raised up.*)

HUMBUG. Where did everyone go?

MATHEMAGICIAN. Oh, they're still in the mine. I often find that the best way to get from one place to another is to erase everything and start again. Please make yourself at home.

(*They find themselves in a very unique room, in which all the walls, tables, chairs, desks, cabinets and blackboards are labeled to show their heights, widths, depths and distances to and from each other. To one side is a gigantic notepad on an artist's easel, and from hooks and strings hang a collection of rulers, measures, weights and tapes, and all other measuring devices.*)

MILO. Do you always travel that way? (*He looks around in wonder.*)

MATHEMAGICIAN. No, indeed! (*He pulls a plumb line from a hook and walks.*) Most of the time I take the shortest distance between any two points. And of course, when I have to be in several places at once . . . (*He writes* $3 \times 1 = 3$ *on the notepad with his staff.*) I simply multiply. (THREE FIGURES *looking like the* MATHEMAGICIAN *appear on a platform above.*)

MILO. How did you do that?

MATHEMAGICIAN AND THE THREE. There's nothing to it, if you have a magic staff. (THE THREE *cancel themselves out and disappear.*)

HUMBUG. That's nothing but a big pencil.

MATHEMAGICIAN. True enough, but once you learn to use it, there's no end to what you can do.

MILO. Can you make things disappear?

MATHEMAGICIAN. Just step a little closer and watch this. (*Shows them that there is nothing up his sleeve or in his hat. He writes:*) $4+9-2\times16+1=3\times6-67+8\times2-3+26-1-34+3-7+2-5=$ (*He looks up expectantly.*)

HUMBUG. Seventeen?

MILO. It all comes to zero.

MATHEMAGICIAN. Precisely. (*Makes a theatrical bow and rips off paper from notepad.*) Now, is there anything else you'd like to see? (*At this point, an appeal to the audience to see if anyone would like a problem solved.*)

MILO. Well . . . can you show me the biggest number there is?

MATHEMAGICIAN. Why, I'd be delighted. (*Opening a closet door.*) We keep it right here. It took four miners to dig it out. (*He shows them a huge "3" twice as high as the* MATHEMAGICIAN.)

MILO. No, that's not what I mean. Can you show me the longest number there is?

MATHEMAGICIAN. Sure. (*Opens another door.*) Here it is. It took three carts to carry it here. (*Door reveals an "8" that is as wide as the "3" was high.*)

MILO. No, no, that's not what I meant either. (*Looks helplessly at* TOCK.)

TOCK. I think what you would like to see is the number of the greatest possible magnitude.

MATHEMAGICIAN. Well, why didn't you say so? (*He busily measures them and all other things as he speaks, and marks it down.*) What's the greatest number you can think of? (*Here, an appeal can also be made to the audience or* MILO *may think of his own answers.*)

MILO. Uh . . . nine trillion, nine hundred and ninety-nine billion, nine hundred ninety-nine million, nine-hundred ninety-nine thousand, nine hundred and ninety-nine. (*He puffs.*)

MATHEMAGICIAN. (*Writes that on the pad.*) Very good. Now add one to it. (MILO *or audience does.*) Now add one again. (MILO *or audience does so.*) Now add one again. Now add one again. Now add . . .

MILO. But when can I stop?

MATHEMAGICIAN. Never. Because the number you want is always at least one more than the number you have, and it's so large that if you started saying it yesterday, you wouldn't finish tomorrow.

HUMBUG. Where could you ever find a number so big?

MATHEMAGICIAN. In the same place they have the smallest number there is, and you know what that is?

MILO. The smallest number . . . let's see . . . one one-millionth?

MATHEMAGICIAN. Almost. Now all you have to do is divide that in half and then divide that in half and then divide that in half and then divide that . . .

MILO. Doesn't that ever stop either?

MATHEMAGICIAN. How can it when you can always take half of what you have and divide it in half again? Look. (*Pointing offstage.*) You see that line?

MILO. You mean that long one out there?

MATHEMAGICIAN. That's it. Now, if you just follow that line forever, and when you reach the end, turn left, you will find the Land of Infinity. That's where the tallest, the shortest, the biggest, the smallest and the most and the least of everything are kept.

MILO. But how can you follow anything forever? You know, I get the feeling that everything in Digitopolis is very difficult.

MATHEMAGICIAN. But on the other hand, I think you'll find that the only thing you can do easily is be wrong, and that's hardly worth the effort.

MILO. But . . . what bothers me is . . . well, why is it that even when things are correct, they don't really seem to be right?

MATHEMAGICIAN. (*Grows sad and quiet.*) How true. It's been that way ever since Rhyme and Reason were banished. (*Sadness turns to fury.*) *And all because of that stubborn wretch Azaz!* It's all his fault.

MILO. Maybe if you discussed it with him . . .

MATHEMAGICIAN. He's just too unreasonable! Why just last month, I sent him a very friendly letter, which he never had the courtesy to answer. See for yourself. (*Puts the letter on the easel. The letter reads:*)

4738 1919,
667 394107 5841 62589
85371 14 39588 7190434 203
27689 57131 481206.

5864 98053,
62179875073

MILO. But maybe he doesn't understand numbers.

MATHEMAGICIAN. Nonsense! Everybody understands numbers. No matter what language you speak, they always mean the same thing. A seven is a seven everywhere in the world.

MILO. (*To* TOCK *and* HUMBUG.) Everyone is so sensitive about what he knows best.

TOCK. With your permission, sir, we'd like to rescue Rhyme and Reason.

MATHEMAGICIAN. Has Azaz agreed to it?

TOCK. Yes, sir.

MATHEMAGICIAN. THEN I DON'T! Ever since they've been banished, we've never agreed on anything, and we never will.

MILO. Never?

MATHEMAGICIAN. NEVER! And if you can prove otherwise, you have my permission to go.

MILO. Well then, with whatever Azaz agrees, you disagree:

MATHEMAGICIAN. Correct.

MILO. And with whatever Azaz disagrees, you agree.

MATHEMAGICIAN. (*Yawning, cleaning his nails.*) Also correct.

MILO. Then, each of you agree that he will disagree with whatever each of you agrees with, and if you both disagree with the same thing, aren't you really in agreement?

MATHEMAGICIAN. I'VE BEEN TRICKED! (*Figures it over, but comes up with the same answer.*)

TOCK. And now may we go?

MATHEMAGICIAN. (*Nods weakly.*) It's a long and dangerous journey. Long before you find them, the demons will know you're there. Watch out for them, because if you ever come face to face, it will be too late. But there is one other obstacle even more serious than that.

MILO. (*Terrified.*) What is it?

MATHEMAGICIAN. I'm afraid I can't tell you until you return. But maybe I can give you something to help you out. (*Claps hands. ENTER the* DODECAHEDRON, *carrying something on a pillow. The* MATHEMAGICIAN *takes it.*) Here is your own magic staff. Use it well and there is nothing it can't do for you. (*Puts a small, gleaming pencil in* MILO'S *breast pocket.*)

HUMBUG. Are you sure you can't tell about that serious obstacle?

MATHEMAGICIAN. Only when you return. And now the Dodecahedron will escort you to the road that leads to the Castle-in-the-Air. Farewell, my friends, and good luck to you. (*They shake hands, say goodbye, and the* DODECAHEDRON *leads them off.*) Good luck to you! (*To himself.*) Because you're sure going to need it. (*He watches them through a telescope and marks down the calculations.*)

DODECAHEDRON. (*He re-enters.*) Well, they're on their way.

MATHEMAGICIAN. So I see. (DODECAHEDRON *stands waiting.*) Well, what is it?

DODECAHEDRON. I was just wondering myself, your

Numbership. What actually *is* the serious obstacle you were talking about?

MATHEMAGICIAN. (*Looks at him in surprise.*) You mean you really don't know?

BLACKOUT

ACT TWO

SCENE 2

THE LAND OF IGNORANCE.

LIGHTS UP on RHYME *and* REASON, *in their castle, looking out two windows.*

RHYME.
I'm worried sick, I must confess
I wonder if they'll have success
All the others tried in vain,
And were never seen or heard again.

REASON. Now, Rhyme, there's no need to be so pessimistic. Milo, Tock, and Humbug have just as much chance of succeeding as they do of failing.

RHYME.
But the demons are so deadly smart
They'll stuff your brain and fill your heart
With petty thoughts and selfish dreams
And trap you with their nasty schemes.

REASON. Now, Rhyme, be reasonable, won't you? And calm down, you always talk in couplets when you get nervous. Milo has learned a lot from his journey. I think he's a match for the demons and that he might soon be knocking at our door. Now come on, cheer up, won't you?

RHYME. I'll try.

(*LIGHTS FADE on the* PRINCESSES *and COME UP on the little Car, traveling slowly.*)

MILO. So this is the Land of Ignorance. It's so dark. I can hardly see a thing. Maybe we should wait until morning.

VOICE. They'll be mourning for you soon enough. (*They look up and see a large, soiled, ugly* BIRD *with a dangerous beak and a malicious expression.*)

MILO. I don't think you understand. We're looking for a place to spend the night.

BIRD. (*Shrieking.*) It's not yours to spend!

MILO. That doesn't make any sense, you see . . .

BIRD. Dollars or cents, it's still not yours to spend.

MILO. But I don't mean . . .

BIRD. Of course you're mean. Anybody who'd spend a night that doesn't belong to him is very mean.

TOCK. Must you interrupt like that?

BIRD. Naturally, it's my job. I take the words right out of your mouth. Haven't we met before? I'm the Everpresent Wordsnatcher.

MILO. Are you a demon?

BIRD. I'm afraid not. I've tried, but the best I can manage to be is a nuisance. (*Suddenly gets nervous as he looks beyond the three.*) And I don't have time to waste with you. (*Starts to leave.*)

TOCK. What is it? What's the matter?

MILO. Hey, don't leave. I wanted to ask you some questions. . . . Wait!

BIRD. Weight? Twenty-seven pounds. Bye-bye. (*Disappears.*)

MILO. Well, he was no help.

MAN. Perhaps I can be of some assistance to you? (*There appears a beautifully-dressed* MAN, *very polished and clean.*) Hello, little boy. (*Shakes* MILO's *hand.*) And how's the faithful dog? (*Pats* TOCK.) And who is this handsome creature? (*Tips his hat to* HUMBUG.)

HUMBUG. (*To others.*) What a pleasant surprise to meet someone so nice in a place like this.

MAN. But before I help you out, I wonder if first you could spare me a little of your time, and help me with a few small jobs?

HUMBUG. Why, certainly.

TOCK. Gladly.

MILO. Sure, we'd be happy to.

MAN. Splendid, for there are just three tasks. First, I would like to move this pile of sand from here to there. (*Indicates through pantomime a large pile of sand.*) But I'm afraid that all I have is this tiny tweezers. (*Hands it to* MILO, *who begins moving the sand one grain at a time.*) Second, I would like to empty this well and fill that other, but I have no bucket, so you'll have to use this eyedropper. (*Hands it to* TOCK, *who begins to work.*) And finally, I must have a hole in this cliff, and here is a needle to dig it. (HUMBUG *eagerly begins. The* MAN *leans against a tree and stares vacantly off into space. The LIGHTS indicate the passage of time.*)

MILO. You know something? I've been working steadily for a long time, now, and I don't feel the least bit tired or hungry. I could go right on the same way forever.

MAN. Maybe you will. (*He yawns.*)

MILO. (*Whispers to* TOCK.) Well, I wish I knew how long it was going to take.

TOCK. Why don't you use your magic staff and find out?

MILO. (*Takes out pencil and calculates to* MAN.) Pardon me, sir, but it's going to take 837 years to finish these jobs.

MAN. Is that so? What a shame. Well then you'd better get on with them.

MILO. But . . . it hardly seems worthwhile.

MAN. WORTHWHILE! Of course they're not worthwhile. I wouldn't ask you to do anything that was worthwhile.

TOCK. Then why bother?

MAN. Because, my friends, what could be more important than doing unimportant things? If you stop to do enough of them, you'll never get where you are going. (*Laughs villainously.*)

MILO. (*Gasps.*) Oh, no. You must be . . .

MAN. Quite correct! I am the Terrible Trivium, demon of petty tasks and worthless jobs, ogre of wasted effort and monster of habit. (*They start to back away from him.*) Don't try to leave, there's so much to do, and you still have 837 years to go on the first job.

MILO. But why do unimportant things?

MAN. Think of all the trouble it saves. If you spend all your time doing only the easy and useless jobs, you'll never have time to worry about the important ones which are so difficult. (*Walks toward them, whispering.*) Now do come and stay with me. We'll have such fun together. There are things to fill and things to empty, things to take away and things to bring back, things to pick up and things to put down . . . (*They are transfixed by his soothing voice. He is about to embrace them when a* VOICE *screams.*)

VOICE. Run! Run! (*They all wake up and run with*

the Trivium behind. As the VOICE *continues to call out directions, they follow until they lose the Trivium.*) RUN! RUN! This way! This way! Over here! Over here! Up here! Down there! Quick, hurry up!

TOCK. (*Panting.*) I think we lost him.

VOICE. Keep going straight! Keep going straight! Now step up! Now step up!

MILO. Look out! (*They all fall into a Trap.*) But he said "up!"

VOICE. Well, I hope you didn't expect to get anywhere by listening to me.

HUMBUG. We're in a deep pit! We'll never get out of here.

VOICE. That is quite an accurate evaluation of the situation.

MILO. (*Shouting angrily.*) Then why did you help us at all?

VOICE. Oh, I'd do as much for anybody. Bad advice is my specialty. (*A Little Furry Creature appears.*) I'm the demon of Insincerity. I don't mean what I say; I don't mean what I do; and I don't mean what I am.

MILO. Then why don't you go away and leave us alone!

INSINCERITY. (VOICE.) Now, there's no need to get angry. You're a very clever boy and I have complete confidence in you. You can certainly climb out of that pit . . . come on, try . . .

MILO. I'm not listening to one word you say! You're just telling me what you think I'd *like* to hear, and not what is important.

INSINCERITY. Well, if that's the way you feel about it . . .

MILO. That's the way I feel about it. We will manage by ourselves without any unnecessary advice from you.

INSINCERITY. (*Stamping his foot.*) Well, all right for you! Most people listen to what I say, but if that's the way you feel, then I'll just go home. (*Exits in a huff.*)

HUMBUG. (*Who has been quivering with fright.*) And don't you ever come back! Well, I guess we showed him, didn't we?

MILO. You know something? This place is a lot more dangerous than I ever imagined.

TOCK. (*Who's been surveying the situation.*) I think I figured a way to get out. Here, hop on my back. (MILO *does so.*) Now, you, Humbug, on top of Milo. (*He does so.*) Now hook your umbrella onto that tree and hold on. (*They climb over* HUMBUG, *then pull him up.*)

HUMBUG. (*As they climb.*) Watch it! Watch it, now. Ow, be careful of my back! My back! Easy, easy . . . oh, this is so difficult. Aren't you finished yet?

TOCK. (*As he pulls up* HUMBUG.) There. Now, I'll lead for a while. Follow me, and we'll stay out of trouble. (*They walk and climb higher and higher.*)

HUMBUG. Can't we slow down a little?

TOCK. Something tells me we better reach the Castle-in-the-Air as soon as possible, and not stop to rest for a single moment. (*They speed up.*)

MILO. What is it, Tock? Did you see something?

TOCK. Just keep walking and don't look back.

MILO. You *did* see something!

HUMBUG. What is it? Another demon?

TOCK. Not just one, I'm afraid. If you want to see what I'm talking about, then turn around. (*They turn around. The stage darkens and hundreds of Yellow Gleaming Eyes can be seen.*)

HUMBUG. Good grief! Do you see how many there are? Hundreds! The Overbearing Know-it-all, the

Gross Exaggeration, the Horrible Hopping Hindsight, . . . and look over there! The Triple Demons of Compromise! Let's get out of here! (*Starts to scurry.*) Hurry up, you two! Must you be so slow about everything?

MILO. Look! There it is, up ahead! The Castle-in-the-Air! (*They all run.*)

HUMBUG. They're gaining!

MILO. But there it is!

HUMBUG. I see it! I see it!

(*They reach the first step and are stopped by a little man in a frock coat, sleeping on a worn ledger. He has a long quill pen and a bottle of ink at his side. He is covered with ink stains over his clothes and wears spectacles.*)

TOCK. Shh! Be very careful. (*They try to step over him, but he wakes up.*)

SENSES TAKER. (*From sleeping position.*) Names? (*He sits up.*)

HUMBUG. Well, I . . .

SENSES TAKER. *NAMES?* (*He opens book and begins to write, splattering himself with ink.*)

HUMBUG. Uh . . . Humbug, Tock and this is Milo.

SENSES TAKER. Splendid, splendid. I haven't had an "M" in ages.

MILO. What do you want our names for? We're sort of in a hurry.

SENSES TAKER. Oh, this won't take long. I'm the official Senses Taker and I must have some information before I can take your sense. Now if you'll just tell me: (*Handing them a form to fill. Speaking slowly and deliberately.*) When you were born, where you were born, why you were born, how old you are now, how old you were then, how old you'll be in a little while . . .

MILO. I wish he'd hurry up. At this rate, the demons will be here before we know it!

SENSES TAKER. . . . Your mother's name, your father's name, where you live, how long you've lived there, the schools you've attended, the schools you haven't attended . . .

HUMBUG. I'm getting writer's cramp.

TOCK. I smell something very evil and it's getting stronger every second. (*To* SENSES TAKER.) May we go now?

SENSES TAKER. Just as soon as you tell me your height, your weight, the number of books you've read this year . . .

MILO. We have to go!

SENSES TAKER. All right, all right, I'll give you the short form. (*Pulls out a small piece of paper.*) Destination?

MILO. But we have to . . .

SENSES TAKER. *DESTINATION?*

MILO, TOCK and HUMBUG. The Castle-in-the-Air! (*They throw down their papers and run past him up the first few stairs.*)

SENSES TAKER. Stop! I'm sure you'd rather see what I have to show you. (*Snaps his fingers; they freeze.*) A circus of your very own. (*CIRCUS MUSIC is heard.* MILO *seems to go into a trance.*) And wouldn't you enjoy this most wonderful smell? (TOCK *sniffs and goes into a trance.*) And here's something I know you'll enjoy hearing . . . (*To* HUMBUG. *The sound of CHEERS and APPLAUSE for* HUMBUG *is heard, and he goes into a trance.*) There we are. And now, I'll just sit back and let the demons catch up with you.

(MILO *accidentally drops his package of gifts. The Package of Laughter from* DR. DISCHORD *opens and the Sounds of Laughter are heard. After a moment,* MILO, TOCK *and* HUMBUG *join in laughing and the spells are broken.*)

MILO. There was no circus.

TOCK. There were no smells.

HUMBUG. The applause is gone.

SENSES TAKER. I warned you I was the Senses Taker. I'll steal your sense of your sense of Purpose, your sense of Duty, destroy your sense of Proportion—and but for one thing, you'd be helpless yet.

MILO. What's that?

SENSES TAKER. As long as you have the sound of laughter, I cannot take your sense of Humor. Agh! That horrible sense of humor.

HUMBUG. HERE THEY COME! LET'S GET OUT OF HERE!

(*The demons appear in nasty slithering hordes, running through the audience and up onto the stage, trying to attack* TOCK, MILO *and* HUMBUG. *The three heroes run past the* SENSES TAKER *up the stairs toward the Castle-in-the-Air with the demons snarling behind them.*)

MILO. Don't look back! Just keep going! (*They reach the castle. The two* PRINCESSES *appear in the windows.*)

PRINCESSES. Hurry! Hurry! We've been expecting you.

MILO. You must be the Princesses. We've come to rescue you.

HUMBUG. And the demons are close behind!

TOCK. We should leave right away.

PRINCESSES. We're ready anytime you are.

MILO. Good, now if you'll just come out. But wait a minute—there's no door! How can we rescue you from the Castle-in-the-Air if there's no way to get in or out?

HUMBUG. Hurry, Milo! They're gaining on us.

REASON. Take your time, Milo, and think about it.

MILO. Ummm, all right . . . just give me a second or two. (*He thinks hard.*)

HUMBUG. I think I feel sick.

MILO. I've got it! Where's that package of presents? (*Opens the package of letters.*) Ah, here it is. (*Takes out the letters and sticks them on the door, spelling:*) E-N-T-R-A-N-C-E. Entrance. Now, let's see. (*Rummages through and spells in smaller letters:*) P-u-s-h. Push. (*He pushes and a door opens. The* PRINCESSES *come out of the castle. Slowly, the demons ascend the stairway.*)

HUMBUG. Oh, it's too late. They're coming up and there's no other way down!

MILO. Unless . . . (*Looks at* TOCK.) Well . . . Time flies, doesn't it?

TOCK. Quite often. Hold on, everyone, and I'll take you down.

HUMBUG. Can you carry us all?

TOCK. We'll soon find out. Ready or not, here we go!

(*His alarm begins to ring. They jump off the platform and disappear. The demons, howling with rage, reach the top and find no one there. They see the* PRINCESSES *and the heroes running across the stage and bound down the stairs after them and into the audience. There is a mad chase scene until they reach the stage again.*)

HUMBUG. I'm exhausted! I can't run another step.

MILO. We can't stop now . . .

TOCK. Milo! Look out there! (*The armies of* AZAZ *and* MATHEMAGICIAN *appear at the back of the theatre, with the Kings at their heads.*)

AZAZ. (*As they march toward the stage.*) Don't worry, Milo, we'll take over now.

MATHEMAGICIAN. Those demons may not know it, but their days are numbered!

SPELLING BEE. Charge! C-H-A-R-G-E! Charge! (*They rush at the demons and battle until the demons run off howling. Everyone cheers. The* FIVE MINISTERS OF AZAZ *appear and shake* MILO'S *hand.*)

MINISTER 1. Well done.

MINISTER 2. Fine job.

MINISTER 3. Good work!

MINISTER 4. Congratulations!

MINISTER 5. CHEERS! (*Everyone cheers again. A fanfare interrupts. A* PAGE *steps forward and reads from a large scroll:*)

PAGE.

Henceforth, and forthwith,
Let it be known by one and all,
That Rhyme and Reason
Reign once more in Wisdom.

(*The* PRINCESSES *bow gratefully and kiss their brothers, the Kings.*)

And furthermore,
The boy named Milo,
The dog known as Tock,
And the insect hereinafter referred to as the Humbug
Are hereby declared to be
Heroes of the Realm.

(*All bow and salute the heroes.*)

MILO. But we never could have done it without a lot of help.

REASON. That may be true, but you had the courage to try, and what you can do is often a matter of what you *will* do.

AZAZ. That's why there was one very important thing about your quest we couldn't discuss until you returned.

MILO. I remember. What was it?

AZAZ. Very simple. It was impossible!

MATHEMAGICIAN. *Completely* impossible!

HUMBUG. Do you mean . . . ? (*Feeling faint.*) Oh, . . . I think I need to sit down.

AZAZ. Yes, indeed, but if we'd told you then, you might not have gone.

MATHEMAGICIAN. And, as you discovered, many things are possible just as long as you don't know they're impossible.

MILO. I think I understand.

RHYME. I'm afraid it's time to go now.

REASON. And you must say goodbye.

MILO. To everyone? (*Looks around at the crowd. To* TOCK *and* HUMBUG.) Can't you two come with me?

HUMBUG. I'm afraid not, old man. I'd like to, but I've arranged for a lecture tour which will keep me occupied for years.

TOCK. And they do need a watchdog here.

MILO. Well, O.K., then. (MILO *hugs the* HUMBUG.)

HUMBUG. (*Sadly.*) Oh, bah.

MILO. (*He hugs* TOCK, *and then faces everyone.*) Well, goodbye. We all spent so much time together, I know I'm going to miss you. (*To the* PRINCESSES.)

I guess we would have reached you a lot sooner if I hadn't made so many mistakes.

REASON. You must never feel badly about making mistakes, Milo, as long as you take the trouble to learn from them. Very often you learn more by being wrong for the right reasons than you do by being right for the wrong ones.

MILO. But there's so much to learn.

RHYME. That's true, but it's not just learning that's important. It's learning what to do with what you learn and learning why you learn things that matters.

MILO. I think I know what you mean, Princess. At least, I hope I do. (*The car is rolled forward and* MILO *climbs in.*) Goodbye! Goodbye! I'll be back someday! I will! Anyway, I'll try. (*As* MILO *drives, the set of the Land of Ignorance begins to move offstage.*)

AZAZ. Goodbye! Always remember. Words! Words! Words!

MATHEMAGICIAN. *And* numbers!

AZAZ. Now, don't tell me you think numbers are as important as words?

MATHEMAGICIAN. Is that so? Why I'll have you know . . . (*The set disappears, and* MILO'S *Room is seen onstage.*)

MILO. (*As he drives on.*) Oh, oh, I hope they don't start all over again. Because I don't think I'll have much time in the near future to help them out. (*The sound of loud ticking is heard.* MILO *finds himself in his room. He gets out of the car and looks around.*)

THE CLOCK. Did someone mention time?

MILO. Boy, I must have been gone for an awful long time. I wonder what time it is. (*Looks at* CLOCK.) Five o'clock. I wonder what day it is. (*Looks at calendar.*) It's still today! I've only been gone for an hour! (*He continues to look at his calendar, and then begins *to look at his books and toys and maps and chemistry set with great interest.*)

CLOCK. An hour. Sixty minutes. How long it really lasts depends on what you do with it. For some people, an hour seems to last forever. For others, just a moment, and so full of things to do.

MILO. (*Looks at clock.*) Six o'clock already?

CLOCK. In an instant. In a trice. Before you have time to blink. (*The stage goes black in less than no time at all.*)

THE END

TALES OF CUSTARD THE DRAGON
Music by Brad Ross
Lyrics by Danny Whitman
Book Adapted by Mary Hall Surface

Family Musical / 4m, 2f, with doubling / Unit Set
Join Custard the Dragon and his friends as they embark on a musical journey in which a most unlikely hero finds true courage. Based on the whimsical stories by Ogden Nash, this musical tale follows the exploits of young Belinda and her three boastfully brave pets, Mustard the Dog, Ink the Cat, and Blink the Mouse, and one not-so-brave dragon, Custard. Yet when Belinda is confronted first by a fearsome pirate and then a wicked knight, it's Cowardly Custard who comes to the rescue. Audiences will treasure Custard's discovery that you can be brave, even when you are afraid – Real courage comes from love. Audiences ages 5 and above will delight in this family musical commissioned and originally produced by the John F. Kennedy Center for the Performing Arts in Washington, DC.

" A masterful musical adaptation of Nash's classic that will delight both the young and the young at heart!" - Derek Gordon, Vice-President for Education (92 - 04), Kennedy Center

UNCLE PIRATE
Book by Ben H. Winters
Music and Lyrics by Drew Fornarola
Based on the Book Uncle Pirate by Douglas Rees

Young Audiences / 3m, 3f

With help from Uncle Pirate and his faithful talking penguin, maybe, just maybe, Wilson can survive the fourth grade. Wilson is just your average kid. Then one day he finds out his uncle is a pirate... like, a REAL pirate! Grab yer eye patches and pirate hats, mateys! The adventure begins now!

"At heart Uncle Pirate proves more of a Boy Scout than a buccaneer, but that won't distress theatergoers under 12, this diverting and often funny musical's ideal audience... Theatergoers at a recent performance particularly enjoyed a classroom duel in which Uncle Pirate bravely wields first a pointer, then a ruler and finally a book. Education, it seems, really is the way to win life's battles."
– *New York Times*

"There's a talking penguin and plenty of 'arrrs!' for the young'uns, while elementary schoolers and their parents will appreciate the sarcastic dialogue and clever songs...a whimsical adaptation of the eponymous kids book is Jolly Roger fun."
– *Time Out New York*

CURIOSITY CAT
Chris Grabenstein

TYA, Young Audience / 6m, 4f, 6 m or f, plus extras

From the imaginative mind of award winning TYA author Chris Grabenstein comes a very funny, very touching new comedy filled with laughter, learning, and heart that's ideal for school groups and professional children's theatres.Curiosity Cat is the play-within-the-book from Grabenstein's award-winning novel for middle grades readers The Hanging Hill. It's a story bout displaced children and homeless cats as well as family and the value of curiosity.

When their mother becomes very ill Claire and Charlie are forced to live with their father's Aunt Jenny. A stray cat named Curiosity also wanders into the house. When he breaks Claire's prized music box, she immediately throws him back out into the streets. Being homeless is an adventure, not a concern, for a cat this curious and cool. Soon, the children (with Fred the dog) set out to rescue Curiosity Cat who is busily trying to help other forlorn felines find homes while simultaneously avoiding a newly appointed "cat catcher" who vows to put him to sleep!

Filled with memorable characters – such as Coot, the geriatric cat; Slicker the big city alley cat; Penelope, the pampered Persian Princess; Fred the extremely loyal dog; a nervous and nutty squirrel; a chorus of cute jailbird strays; and the evil cat catcher Skeevelberger – the play builds to a funny and touching climax that will leave audiences laughing and cheering!

A NUTTY NUTCRACKER CHRISTMAS
Ralph Covert and G. Riley Mills

Holiday / 5m, 6f plus chorus

A rockin' holiday treat from Ralph Covert of "Ralph's World" and Jeff Award winning playwright G. Riley Mills. A Nutty Nutcracker Christmas is a fun, fresh holiday spectacular for the entire family. Boasting holiday hits like "Welcome to Christmas Wood," "The Wind-Up Toy Ballet," and crowd favorite "Let's Ruin Christmas," this rockin' contemporary adaptation follows Fritz and the Nutcracker through Christmas Wood. When trouble arises with the dastardly Mouse King, Fritz and Nutcracker must save the day.

"Top 10 Holiday Show Pick!"
– *Chicago Tribune*

MIDNIGHT RIDE OF PAUL REVERE
Book and Lyrics by Ben H. Winters
Music and Lyrics by Stephen Sislen

5m, 1f, with doubling, expandable cast / Unit Set

In Boston, Paul Revere etches out a humble living as a silversmith. Americans and British alike hail the exquisite artistry of his work. But when Paul's revolutionary friends, John Hancock and Samuel Adams pressure Revere to take a stand against British tyranny and join the Sons of Liberty, he worries that supporting the cause of revolution would mean losing his business and risking the safety of his family. Revere must make a choice: to do what is easy, or to do what is right. From the halls of British Parliament, to the port of Boston and the "Tea Party" protest, to the Boston Massacre and the dangerous thrill of Revere's now-legendary ride, this new musical makes American history accessible and exciting through a unique combination of music, drama and humor. The Midnight Ride of Paul Revere tells the inspirational, universal story of how ordinary people can make a difference.

CPSIA information can be obtained
at www.ICGtesting.com
Printed in the USA
BVOW06s0712230817
492797BV00011B/76/P